To the Rescue!

"Look out! Jim, get them—stop them!" Elly Mae's voice rose to a scream. The plant was threshing back and forth wildly. He could feel the fear and pain it broadcast. There was movement in the water. The crabs were back! They were attacking the plants' roots.

Jim looked about wildly for a weapon. If he had even a club! The plant was twitching, and Elly Mae had reached out her hands to it. Those green cords which had drawn it to them snapped out, fastened on the girl's arms and hands. She pulled back and the plant followed her farther and farther out of the water. A thick root was exposed. To the bits of it which projected on either side clung the crabs, slashing.

Jim crouched past Elly Mae and the struggling plant to kick out at the crabs. He shouted as he beat at them....

STAR KA'ATS AND THE PLANT PEOPLE

ANDRE NORTON & DOROTHY MADLEE

AN ARCHWAY PAPERBACK
POCKET BOOKS . NEW YORK

POCKET BOOKS, a Simon & Schuster division of GULF & WESTERN CORPORATION
1230 Avenue of the Americas, New York, N.Y. 10020

Text copyright © 1979 by Andre Norton and Dorothy Madlee
Illustrations copyright © 1979 by Jean Jenkins Loewer

Published by arrangement with Walker & Company
Library of Congress Catalog Card Number: 78-67177

ISBN: 0-671-56045-X

First Pocket Books printing May, 1980

10 9 8 7 6 5 4 3 2 1

AN ARCHWAY PAPERBACK and ARCH are trademarks
of Simon & Schuster

Printed in the U.S.A.

Contents

1

Trouble in the Air

ELLY MAE gripped the back of the seat in front of her so tightly that her fingers ached. There was something wrong with the flyer. It was wobbling back and forth. She could tell from the way Tiro was hunched over in the seat ahead that the big Ka'at was frightened, too. They had started to the City of the People this morning, and then this had happened. Now the flyer shook and quivered and made snarling sounds.

Elly Mae sensed that Tiro was *thinking* at the machine, trying to keep the engine going. No—he was trying to think it down to the ground.

1

"What's the matter?" The boy on the seat beside her leaned far forward. His hands went out as if he wanted to reach right over Tiro and grab the hand controls that the Ka'ats never used.

"Don't!" Elly Mae screamed. "He's tryin' to get us down!" She swallowed, though her mouth was all dry inside.

She could feel Jim shaking because her shoulder rubbed against his in the Ka'at seats that were not quite wide enough for children. She remembered something now: Jim's mom and dad had been killed in a falling plane back on that other world, which now seemed so far away.

"We've got to land!" Jim's voice was as loud as hers had been. He tried to reach past Tiro, but Mer, sitting beside the Ka'at scout, growled and raked claws along the boy's outstretched hand.

Elly Mae wanted to close her eyes but she could not. She would not, however, look down towards the ground. The way they were swooping made her sick to her stomach. Why wouldn't the flyer respond

2

to Tiro's thought-commands as it always had before? The Ka'ats made all their machines work by a process of think-send. Why wouldn't this one obey?

The shaking became worse. It banged Elly Mae against Jim and then against the side. She tried to hold on tighter.

Once more they swooped. Were they going to crash? There were stories about flyers that had gone out and never returned—or that had been found as crumpled wreckage with the Ka'ats who had trusted them dead or badly hurt.

It was because of the flyers that they were going to the deserted City. The Ka'ats could operate the People's flyers, but they needed to find metal for repairs and re-placements.

The flyer seemed to give a twist, as if it were going to break apart. Then there was a thump and Elly Mae was thrown forward as the flyer came to a stop.

Somehow they got out. Elly Mae kept rubbing her arms and legs which were shaking hard. There was the comforting

3

feel of her soft, furry suit. Touching that was like running her hands down Mer's smooth back. Only her suit did not purr. Mer. . . .

She glanced quickly around for the Ka'at with the smudgy white fur and the strange blue eyes. Mer was there, looking just like always—like a cat. Elly Mae had once thought she *was* an earth cat, just as Jim had believed Tiro, the green eyed, shining black Ka'at, was somebody's lost pet.

Then they had learned that they were not pets at all. They were Ka'ats, scouts from a space ship sent to gather their kindred, the cats of earth, and fly them home. And Elly Mae and Jim had been allowed to come along because Mer and Tiro had spoken up for them.

Elly Mae drew a deep breath and Mer came to her, rubbing against her comfortingly. Tiro was stalking around the flyer. He lashed his long tail angrily, and it seemed that when he looked at the machine his eyes shot sparks.

Jim was breathing fast. His face was

4

very pale. Elly Mae put out her hand and touched his arm. He stared back at her as if he were mad enough to spit—just the way Tiro looked. Maybe he did not want her to know he was afraid. But anyone would be afraid! Elly Mae wanted to say that. But before she could, Tiro mind-spoke:

"We have been lucky indeed. This is another of the metal dead ships. . . ."

It was Micha, a slim red Ka'at now waiting for them in the City, who had talked about metal dead ships. Something had happened to machines that were used too long. They might suddenly come apart. The metal itself became weak.

Once more Elly Mae wiped her hands down her sides. She was not frightened—at least not as much as before—but her legs still felt shaky.

"We are very near the City," that was Mer's thought. "Perhaps we should go in that direction."

"Well enough," agreed Tiro.

Jim, as if he were doing something very hard for him, had gone back to the flyer to

5

drag out their supply bags. He shouldered one and Elly Mae went to pick up the other. Her hands did not shake so much now.

Her hands—that was why she and Jim went to the City each day. Because Tiro and Mer, and the rest of the Ka'ats, no matter how clever they were at mind-sending and running their own machines, did not have hands—but paws. The City had been built by people, like Jim and Elly, and *their* machines were for hands. Those people had been gone a long time but their things were still here and the Ka'ats needed to know more about them.

"We must learn quickly where fresh metal can be found," Tiro was still inspecting the downed flyer. "The supplies we have left are very low. No more flyers can be built now."

"It's like a treasure hunt," Jim said as he settled his supply bag between his shoulders.

It was not only the flyers that were failing. The feeder machines were also breaking down. For a long time the Ka'ats had used supplies of metal left by the People to make new machines and to repair the old. But now that supply was nearly gone and it was important to learn where it had come from.

The four of them tramped across the land towards the big gray City. Elly Mae hated the place. It had been a trap once. She and Jim had found Tiro and Mer caught there. And it was sheer luck which had enabled them to turn the City off and stop the robots left as guards. Every time she went there, Elly Mae secretly expected one of those robots to come marching along to capture them again.

She hurried as they went down one street and then another. At least Jim and Tiro and Mer were with her. Even so, she kept looking up and around.

Now they reached the big centermost building where Mer and Tiro had been in the death cages and where she and Jim had turned off the source of power. Vocal sounds had made one of the robots stop just as it was going to use the force to

7

kill the Ka'ats. Just recently they had discovered that sounds could also make some of the machines go again.

That, too, they had discovered by accident. Elly Mae had been so mad at one of the machines they were examining two days ago that she had kicked it and shouted out some bad names to call it. Then the machine had come to life and small swirly marks had flashed onto a smooth plate on its front panel.

Jim said it was like TV, and they spent half the day watching it change when Elly Mae yelled at it. But she had to do the yelling in just the right tone of voice. After that, they had gone around shouting, singing, or just plain talking at the machines. A few of them came to life. It was scary in a way. But Mer and Tiro and Micha and some of the other Ka'ats, as well as Jim, had been with her, so she had not been too frightened.

Now she tried to remember the sounds that brought the last machine—the one they had left yesterday—to life. It had been one of those with the swirling writing, but there had been pictures, too. And the Ka'ats were excited over that. Mer thought-talked to say it was a kind of machine that might know about working with metal.

Jim dropped to the floor facing one of the machines. He started hooting just as Ana came in. They had known the big silver-furred Ka'at, one of the leaders, would be coming to meet them in another flyer. Ana listened to Tiro's report about the wrecked flyer, then went to stand on her hind legs, her forepaws resting against the side of the box before Jim, her nose nearly touching it. "This is warm. . . ." Ana's thought came clearly as Elly Mae settled beside the boy. "Therefore the machine must be alive in the manner of those the People made."

"Maybe. . . ." Jim started to say aloud and then put his answer slowly into thought-speech—he found that more difficult than Elly Mae–"it's running all right. But how does it work?" He glanced at Elly Mae. "You want to try?"

9

Jim was frowning and Elly Mae knew that he hated to admit that he could not make this machine work. On his knee he balanced a flat thing he had found in one of the upper rooms and carried around now in his supply bag. It had a surface like a sheet of paper and there had been a kind of pen with it. On it Jim copied down as fast as he could—for the pictures flickered so swiftly by—any signs he thought might be useful.

"You tried loud?" Elly Mae stared at the machine.

"Loud? I almost shouted my head off at it yesterday!" Jim answered. "Dumb old thing! But Ana thinks it may be important because it was set off by itself this way."

Jim was right. Most of the machine-boxes they had been viewing were arranged in rows or in groups. This one stood alone at the end of the room nearest to the doorway.

Mer padded into view. With her was the older Ka'at Micha, who was in charge of running the Ka'at repair robots. With Tiro they sat down quietly, folding the tips of their tails over their paws.

Elly Mae put her hand inside her supply bag and brought out one of the odd-looking burgers in bun which were made by the food machine. She had been eating them now for so many days that they did not even look strange to her anymore. Biting into her lunch, she pushed the bag in Jim's

11

direction and continued to look at the machine.

It was a little larger than the others, and the smooth space on the front which made up the picture screen was bigger, too. That was dark. But Ana said the machine was warm, ready to run. They just had to make the right sounds.

Elly Mae chewed and swallowed a generous bit of burger and bun. She drew a deep breath, then, still holding the burger, she did her own range of squeals, sharp clicking noises, and near shrieks.

The screen remained dark.

"See?" demanded Jim, waving a hand toward the box. "This is one I bet we can't make work. The People must have talked to it. Only we don't know what they said, so we can't. . . ."

Elly Mae stuck her tongue out at the obstinate box. "Mean old thing!" She sometimes felt as if these machines made by the People, were alive in some way, and were just acting stupid to make everything hard.

But Elly Mae was not easily defeated. She never had been. Patiently she thought about the problem as she finished her burger. If this was a more important machine, then there would have been a different way of making it work. Jim had tried all his sounds, she had done most of hers. But there was something that would bring it to life, of that she was sure.

The People had hated the Ka'ats, so that any sound which Ka'ats could make would not put one of the City machines to work. But did the noise have to be a voice? For the first time that thought popped into Elly Mae's mind.

"Quite so," Mer's mind-speech answered. "But what sound, little sister-kin?"

Elly Mae looked to Jim who was still eating and scowling at the box.

"Maybe we ought to try something else—another kind of sound. . . ."

"What kind?" he demanded.

Elly Mae glanced around. In the far corner of the room lay a sprawling tangle

13

of metal rods and the column of a body. That was one of the guardian robots that had "died" when the city had been turned off. Elly Mae went over to it now.

"Can you get this off?" She kneeled to hold up one of the jointed arms as she looked over her shoulder at Jim.

He joined her, taking hold of the arm and waving it back and forth until they heard a faint rasp of metal against metal. "I guess so. What do you want it for?"

"To make a noise. . . ."

Jim pulled open the bag he had brought along and into which he had dropped some small tools and bits of wire and rod he had found during their search of the building. He went to work on the tumbled robot and shortly handed Elly Mae a loose arm.

She was not quite sure just how she was going to use it—not yet. Maybe her idea was no good anyway. But she returned to stand before the box. Now she held out the arm and began to tap gently on the top of the machine. Along with those taps she repeated in a low voice some of the sounds

14

which had worked with other machines before.

As her tapping grew louder and more emphatic, so did the sounds grow louder and higher. They all kept a close watch on the screen but there was no change. The vision plate in front did not light up.

Tap. . . squeak. . . .Then. . . .

"That's it!" Jim hunkered down.

The screen had flashed on, but, as quickly, the light was gone once more.

"Try that again, Elly Mae!"

It took four tries before she hit just the right combination of sounds. This time the screen remained on. There were none of the squiggles which Jim was sure were writing. Instead there were pictures of lines, some curved, some straight. Each held only for the space of a breath or two, and then was gone. Jim thought those were maps.

He had appealed earlier to the Ka'ats when they had seen such pictures on other machines. But Ka'ats were not used to maps. They possessed within themselves a guide to where they were and where home was—even as the cats of his own world had done. They did not need such pictures to aid them in their travels.

Therefore they would not recognize any map. Suddenly Micha spoke. He reared up beside the machine even as Ana had done earlier, and now his slender cream-colored paw shadowed the screen for an instant as he patted its surface.

"It is the metal mark!" His thought-speech came swiftly, and along with the thought he gave a small growl.

Jim hurriedly made lines on his pad. If the picture would only hold! No. . . . it had already flashed off. He was so mad he could have kicked the machine as Elly Mae had done when they had made their first discovery.

Two more pictures and then the screen remained dark. Jim scowled.

"I didn't get it. We've got to see it again."

Elly Mae shaped a thought at Micha. "Elder brother," she was always careful to

use the polite address of the Ka'ats, "what is the metal mark?"

"It is the mark we have found on all the stored metal that we have drawn upon for our repairs, and for the making of new things. That was it on the picture. . . ."

"A map of a mine" Jim spoke before he shaped thought. "We've got to see that again! Can you get it, Elly Mae? Maybe this thing," he pushed out a foot and tapped the machine, "will run it through the same way."

Elly Mae began again the taps of the rod and her squeaking. It was some time before she hit upon the right sound and the pictures flicked. And she had to do it four more times before Jim was sure he had the maps properly copied. Tired out, she slumped to the floor.

"You got your picture map," she said. "Now how are you goin' to find the place? The Ka'ats, they don't use no picture maps."

Jim studied the rough drawing on his board. That was going to be a problem. He

18

bit the top of the strange pen he had been using. Maps—when he and Dad and Mom had gone on a trip in the car they had used maps. There had been dots for cities and towns, and the highways had numbers. What he had drawn here was just a lot of lines with no other markings. Except the one Micha knew because it had been stamped on metal.

That was not at the bottom of the map—but rather to the left-hand side, a little away from a line which curled back and forth from the lower edge of the drawing toward the top. One of the other lines ran to the edge of that wavering one from right to left. The others did not touch either of those first two.

The Ka'ats would not recognize them. How then. . . .

Jim stiffened. There just might be a way. From the air! Things could be seen more clearly from the air when they were hard to make out at ground level. If they could take one of the other flyers and go out and look, they might just find the way to the

19

mines. He did not want to think of going in a flyer again, but there was nothing else to do.

"An excellent suggestion, brother kin." Tiro arose and stretched. "At least we can be out of this place of bad memories for a while." He looked around him with a low-throated growl of hatred for the trap-city of the People. "And be sure our flyer will be well tested."

2

The Sealed Island

IT WAS THE next day before they could get
into the air. Elly Mae wished they could
walk. But when Mer, Tiro and Micha
seemed so confident, she did not want to
say so. Even then they were not sure just
which way to go. Mer and Tiro and Micha
were together in the front seat of a new
and stronger flyer. Elly Mae and Jim
crouched behind to look over their furry
heads. She wondered what Jim thought
about flying, but he just held his drawing
of the map on his knees and kept looking
down as well as he could from the side to
try and pick out something—anything—
that might be like the marks he had

copied. Being so interested in the map kept his thoughts from that forced landing.

They flew a big circle around the City of the People, and then another, each time going farther out at the slowest speed Tiro could hold the flyer to. Soon, as they circled, they had gone so far that they could not see the City—except as a distant spot on the ground.

"How about up in those hills?" Jim wanted to know, pointing over Micha and Mer at the line of heights to the north. "Mines on our world—lots of times they were in mountains." He was trying hard to remember all he had known about mines. But that was very little. And the People here might have had very different ways of obtaining ore.

Tiro sent the flyer toward the mountains. There again they wove a pattern back and forth. But there was nothing to be seen below which looked like Jim's poorly drawn map. Perhaps he had been wrong, he thought unhappily. Perhaps this was not a map at all.

He traced the lines with his fingertip. One of them ran very straight, too straight to be a river. Maybe a road? But he had not seen any roads leading to or from the city. He had thought that the People must have used only flyers to travel.

"A road—if we just saw a road . . . ." he thought and said aloud.

Tiro swung the flyer away from the hills. They headed west now and into Jim's mind came the big Ka'at's thought-send:

"A travel place for the People. There is one such. It leads to the water not to be drunk . . . ."

Jim was puzzled but Tiro did not explain further. He watched eagerly for any sign of a road which might match the line on his map.

"There! Look, Elly Mae . . . there it is!"

They had indeed come to hover over what looked like a road. It was very narrow and shiny. As Tiro made the flyer follow it, they sighted strange-looking round things in the middle that hid the road lines. From the air they looked as if someone had

23

strung a line of big cans together to lie on their sides.

Micha's nose was pressed flat against the bubble cover of the flyer as he started down. "There is no life," he said. "We can descend without fear."

Tiro set the flyer down and they tumbled out in a hurry. On the ground they had to look up to see the tops of those round things. They were made of metal, and there were brown-colored spots running along their sides as if they had begun to rust. They must have been there for a long time. Perhaps ever since the People had sealed the City.

Both Ka'ats and the children had learned to be very careful in approaching anything that had been made by the People. They circled around the cans at a respectful distance.

Elly Mae knew that the Ka'ats could sense traps of the People. So she was willing to wait until Mer and Tiro announced that it was safe. But a moment later, as they came to one end of the round things, she broke out in surprise. "This ain't no road! Look there, will you?"

What had seemed a solid surface from the air was not that. Instead here ran a groove, covered with smooth coating like the metal used everywhere in the City. Now they could also see that the first of the round things had a ridge on its bottom which fitted into the groove.

Jim eyed it carefully. "I think maybe it's some kind of train," he said slowly. "It slipped along here . . . ." He leaned over to look down into the groove, then glanced at the can like things.

Micha was trotting along beside the stalled line.

"The cubling is right," his thought came back. "These were carriers for the People." He went closer to the nearest and sniffed along its side, his red-gold back roughed with excitement. His exploration carried him midway and there he reared on his hind legs to nose at the smooth surface. "An opening here," he announced.

The other four joined him. Jim traced

25

the outline of an oval door that was tightly closed. He laid aside the map and reached up with both hands, pushing at the oval. It was tight shut. He tried to remember how doors in earth trains opened, but he could not. Maybe they needed sounds here, too.

Elly Mae, who had come to join him, had a suggestion. "The doors in the City—you pushed from the side, not from the middle. Maybe this works the same way."

Why hadn't he thought of that? Jim was disturbed that Elly Mae remembered before he did. He quickly changed his place and once more set his hands to push to the left. Elly Mae's brown fingers were flattened beside his own and together they shoved.

There was a grating sound. The door gave a little.

"Push!" Jim ordered. "It's stuck. Been shut so long, I guess."

Push they did with all their strength. The door moved a little, but they could not force it very far. The crack was too narrow

26

for them to get inside. For all their shoving they could open it no wider.

But Micha squeezed in head and shoulders. A moment later his thought-send seemed as loud as a shout in their minds.

"Metal—much metal! This is a great find!"

Jim was panting from the effort of trying to open the door. He wiped his sweating face with his forearm. So what if it was the metal, they hadn't found any mine. He squatted down on the ground to look at the map again.

The Ka'ats were busy at the car—for car it must be, just as these can things must also be a train. They had squeezed through the crack, which was far too narrow for the children, and were examining the find.

"Maybe they can use all this . . ." Jim waved his hand at the six cars as he spoke to Elly Mae, "but it won't last forever. There's just got to be a mine somewhere and we ought to find that."

Elly Mae dropped down beside him, staring at the map. "If this here," her finger

traced the straight line, "is this railroad—then it keeps on running, don't it? An' what's at the ends?"

Jim nodded. "Maybe that way," he pointed. "It connects with the City somehow. Or it did once. So, if there's any mine, it has to be that way . . . ." He half turned his body to point along the track in the opposite direction. "So we ought to go that way."

"We shall, kin-cub." Tiro dropped out of the door crack. "Your reasoning holds promise. Micha wishes to determine how large this newfound treasure is, even though it cannot provide us with all that we need. So let us indeed find its source."

Micha stayed with the stalled train, but the children, with Mer and Tiro, once more took up the flyer. They followed the line of the track until they came upon a shore where waves crashed. Tiro sent the flyer lower.

"Bad water," he announced. "One cannot drink such . . . ."

"A sea!" Jim crowded against the side of the flyer. "And look—those look like boats!"

The grooved track ended in a wide circle. There were more of the round cars here, and several buildings. Though not as large as the buildings in the City, these were made the same way. A wharf ran out into the water. Nudged against it were boats. Only one or two were still afloat. Parts of the hulls of several more showed that quite a few had sunk.

"Out there—there's something out there!" Elly Mae pointed to the sea. "Let's see what that is."

She was right. Jim saw a smudge of darkness on the water. It was queer looking, and half hidden by a fog. From here all he could see was a big dark blot.

Tiro shared Elly Mae's curiosity, for he sent the flyer out over the water, skimming not far above the waves and heading toward that misty place. As they came closer, it appeared bigger and bigger, but the fog was so thick, they could not see any detail.

Suddenly the flier lurched to one side and dropped nearly into the water. Tiro jerked his head and Mer let out a spitting hiss. The flyer sped to the right, turned, and headed back to the shore.

"What's the matter?" Jim demanded, puzzled.

"There is a guard . . . did not you feel it?" Mer asked.

"Didn't feel nothing," Elly Mae answered for both of them. "Was it in your heads?"

"Just so, kin-cub," Mer said. "This is a guard set by the People."

"If they set a guard on it," Jim said, "there must be something important out there." This must be the place from which the cars loaded with the metal had come. If so, then this might be the mine. Except—who ever heard of a mine in a sea?

Tiro, having brought them back to shore, set the flyer down on an open patch of ground just beyond the first of the buildings. They got out and looked around warily. Having known the terrible trap in the City, they were all afraid that something similar might be waiting here also. After a long moment Tiro shook his head.

"This is a dead place," he thought, "there are no machines alive here."

Just the same, Jim believed in being very careful, and he impressed on the Ka'ats the need that he and Elly Mae go

32

first. They had proved that guards set by the People would not bother them, while Tiro and Mer could still be in danger.

In two of the buildings they found piles of metal shaped like bricks. But in the third there were instead big bins filled with bits of metal, some round and the size of marbles, others smaller, hardly as big as shot for a BB gun. There was also something that Jim guessed might be a furnace. Perhaps the bits had been melted down here to form the bricks stored elsewhere.

"A great find," Tiro was excited. "There is enough here to give us all we need right now."

Jim picked up a handful of the metal bits and let them trickle away between his fingers.

"Sure, this will keep things going for a while. But we haven't found the mine. Then we'd always have what was needed. If the mine *is* out there . . ." he nodded at the wall which faced on the sea, "then we should go there, too."

"It is guarded," Mer reminded him.

"Maybe for Ka'ats," Elly Mae spoke up. "But we could go, Jim and me. Maybe there's something there we could bust— like we busted that thing in the city and made all the robots fall dead. Then you could come, too . . . ."

Jim nodded. "It's worth our trying anyway. We can take the flyer and use the hand controls. At least maybe we could see what is there."

Tiro and Mer looked into each other's eyes. They were talking it over, Jim knew, and their thoughts were such now that the children could not pick them up at all. What he had said made sense. If there was a Ka'at barrier out there, it would not keep Elly Mae and him out. They had proved that when they first went into the City. But, at the same time, he wasn't sure he really wanted to go. There was something scary about that foggy place in the sea.

"What you suggest," Tiro now used thought-send that Jim could understand, "has merit. It is true that you can use the hand controls of the flyer as did the People.

Go out then and see what lies there, but do not descend rashly."

"Don't worry," Jim answered, "I'm not going to."

"*We're* not going to." Elly Mae was already heading for the door.

Jim knew better than to try to argue her out of going with him. He suspected that deep down, Elly Mae did not like what they were going to try any more than he did. But she would never consent to staying behind.

The flyer did not rise as smoothly as it had under Tiro's practiced thought-control, but Jim had flown with hand controls before. Soon he had the flyer in the air and heading out to sea. He sent it straight toward the foggy island.

Jim hunched closer to the controls. He had first flown one of these when he and Elly Mae had gone months ago to explore the City of the People. Since then he had practiced many times with the machines which the Ka'ats kept for their use. But he was always uneasy and afraid of making a mistake, though he would not allow Elly Mae to guess that.

"It looks funny . . ." Elly Mae had leaned far forward. "All foggy . . . ."

The closer they came the less they could see. Now the flyer dove into what seemed an unusually thick mist. Jim grew tense. Must not get caught in this stuff and ram against a building—if there were any buildings hidden here.

"Look!" Elly Mae's forehead pressed against the glass. Under them was a slick surface which rounded up like the top of a big bubble. There was no place to land the flyer. What lay below looked like steam-covered glass, just like the top of the flyer cockpit, though many times larger. The fog which surrounded them made drops run down their covering.

Jim sent the flyer back and forth through the mist. There was nothing below but that huge rounded surface. It appeared to cover nearly as much ground as a good half of the City, Jim guessed. There was no place to land and hardly anything to see.

Down beneath the curving surface, there appeared another kind of cloud as thick or thicker than the fog. Whatever might be inside was hidden.

At last he started the flyer back. He and Elly Mae certainly had not . . . .

Jim cried out. The flyer dipped and his hold on the controls faltered. He heard Elly Mae's scream:

"Don't—oh, don't . . . .!"

It wasn't fear of the flyer crashing. It was that other thing—the horrible thing in her head. She clapped both hands to her ears, but that didn't shut out what she heard in her mind.

This was no cry sent by the Ka'ats, it was very different. There *was* something down there—something which was hurting and was afraid—so very much afraid!

3

Cry For Help

JIM FELT IT, too. He shook his head, trying to shut the hurting out. Elly Mae was right! There was something alive down there, and it was afraid and in terrible pain. But it was not a Ka'at. It did not thought-talk like Mer or Tiro. Instead it could only transmit fear and pain. And it needed help!

"We gotta help. . ." Elly Mae held her hands pressed over her ears. She felt so bad inside, like she must do something right away. Only she did not know what was to be done. "We gotta go down there and help. . ."

"We can't land," Jim pointed out.

"There's no place to set the flyer down."

They had skimmed back and forth across the bubble's top. As far as they could see there was no place level enough to land. Because the mist was so thick it was hard to tell what might be farther down.

"It hurts!" Elly Mae rocked back and forth in the too-small seat. "It hurts in my head!"

"I know. . ." Jim had turned the flyer about, and was heading out through the veiling of the mist, back towards the shore.

"We gotta go down an' help!" Elly Mae cried. "You're taking us away!"

He had half-expected, when they at last flew out of the mist, that the feeling in his mind would go away. But, though it was less intense now (more like a person whispering instead of shouting in his ear), he could still sense it.

"Why can't we take one of the boats . . . ." Elly Mae looked down ahead at the wharf and at the boats moored there.

"I doubt that either of them will float," Jim countered. The cry had nearly died away now, and he did not want to feel it again.

"Maybe one will. We have to go—you know we do!"

But he did not want to go back to that big bubble that held whatever bad thing had come into their heads. Jim landed the flyer and they climbed out to face the waiting Ka'ats. Micha, Jim saw, had left the stalled train and joined Mer and Tiro.

Elly Mae's thought-send began even before her feet touched the ground, sharing with Mer and the rest what they had discovered. Her account was as breathless as if she had burst out aloud, one word tumbling over another.

". . . and it's hurt. It needs help . . ."

Mer rubbed around Elly Mae's legs. Her thought-send was soothing.

"Of what manner is it, cubling? Does it use Ka'at talk?"

Both Tiro and Micha regarded the children with unblinking stares. Jim could feel their unvoiced questions. Together he and Elly Mae repeated all they had

41

learned—seeing the bubble-like covering on what must be the island—and that message.

"Not Ka'at," Tiro repeated thoughtfully. "Not the People?"

Jim hunched down on the ground and rubbed one hand across his forehead. Elly Mae, sitting cross-legged a little beyond, stroked Mer, and the white Ka'at reached up a paw to pat her cheek. The boy had not thought of that. Had they caught an appeal from one of the People? But it was supposed to be a long time since they had gathered into their last City and sealed themselves in.

Inside the City now there had been no one left—only the machines and the robots. Could it be that some of the People, even just one or two, still lived out there?

"It thought at us!" Elly Mae answered. "And you said that the People were afraid to thought-talk—that they never did it!"

"True," Tiro said thoughtfully. "And you are sure it was not Ka'at?"

Both children nodded. That cry had been

42

strange. It had not come in real word messages such as the Ka'ats used. Rather it communicated only the feeling of hurt and fear.

"No machine," Micha said. "We have found no machine that could send feelings in this way. But what lies out there?"

Elly Mae rose on her knees. "We have to go and see, we just got to! There's something bad happening and maybe we can help. Maybe we could take one of the boats . . . ." She pointed to the wharf where there were still two boats afloat.

Jim stirred uneasily. Sure, he had felt it, too, but he could foresee all the things that might go wrong. Even if one of those boats would float—how were they going to get it going? He did not know anything about boats.

And, once they got there, suppose there was someone or something waiting for them . . .? He did not have a gun, or anything else he could use as a weapon. To head back was kind of stupid.

Elly Mae caught at his arm.

"Let's go and look at them boats! We gotta go back . . ."

"All right."

They went down to the wharf, the Ka'ats trotting beside them. There had been seven boats here. Two were ashore, their noses rammed high on the land, big dents in their sides. Three had partly sunk so that one could see them under the water, with the waves catching on them as the sea washed back and forth.

Jim stepped out on the wharf cautiously. It appeared to be made of the same metal as the cars, the rail, and much of the sealed city. But there were patches of flaking and he tried to avoid those, fearing that the rust had weakened the surface.

The two boats still afloat were moored one on either side of the wharf. One of them rode deeper in the water. When the children looked down at it they could see it was slowly filling up. To trust to that one would be risky.

Micha had gone on to the other boat and now a thought summoned them.

"This seems to be mostly free of water. It has also the hand controls—like those of the flyer."

He was right. The boat was smaller and, though it had some water in the bottom, there was only a little. There were seats at the forepart similar to those in the flyer, though these were larger and undoubtedly had been made for People. Before the left-hand seat there was a bank of controls like those of the flyer.

Jim, with Elly Mae only a moment behind him, slipped down into the cockpit. There was a large space behind the seats like the body of a truck. The vanished People had probably used this boat to transport something.

The children splashed through the scummy water to the seats. Jim settled in the one before the controls.

"Can you run it?" Elly Mae demanded.

"I don't know." Did the boat have any fuel? Could he steer a boat in the same way as a flyer? He could only try.

A little fearful, he leaned forward and

jerked at a lever which, on a flyer, brought the engine to life. It was stuck and he had to use both hands to work it loose, little by little, until he could pull it back.

For a long moment nothing happened and Jim began to think that, like its makers, the boat engine was dead.

Then there was a spitting noise. The boat shook and came to life. A sobering thought made Jim hesitate. Suppose they started on their way to the island and the engine stopped? Jim could swim a little but he doubted whether Elly Mae could.

But if he had any doubts Elly Mae did not share them. She had already thought-sent to Mer for the Ka'ats to unfasten the mooring chains. Before Jim had time to protest, they were loose in the swing of the waves.

"Hurry up!" Elly Mae ordered. "We've just got to get out there an' help . . . ."

"Help what?" he asked.

Now free, the boat frightened him even more. He tested the controls. They were enough like those of the flyers that he thought he might be able to steer. He hoped so.

"Help that thing!" She was impatient. Her hand jabbed into the air to indicate the island which, from sea level, was just a formless shadow lying on the water.

Jim drew a deep breath and headed the boat out. His whole body was stiff and he tried not to think of what might happen if the engine *did* quit and he and Elly Mae would be unable to get back to shore.

Now and then the engine coughed and spit. Each time Jim was sure it was going to stop altogether, and he held his breath until it started up again. They were moving much slower than the flyer, and pushing against the force of the incoming waves made traveling harder.

He did not want to look back and see the shore so far behind. Though the boat went forward, the island did not appear any larger or clearer. In fact, at sea level the mists around it were even thicker.

Suddenly he lost the desire to turn back.

There was something—a feeling that he must go on. . . .

Elly Mae's hands were on either side of her head, covering her ears. Then Jim caught it, too. Faint now—but growing more intense. There was no fright now—just pain—terrible pain. . . .!

Elly Mae's eyes were squeezed shut. "Hurry!" she cried, "Hurry!"

But there was no hurrying the progress of the boat, though they continued to head towards the island. Then the pitiful call stopped, leaving a queer emptiness and silence in their minds.

Elly Mae dropped her hands. "It's dead," she said in a low voice. "We didn't help it in time and now it's dead!"

Jim agreed with her. Maybe now they could turn back. But when he tried to move the controls, he could do nothing. The boat kept on.

Now the mist reached out for them. Jim fought to move the controls. If they kept on this way, blinded by the fog, they might well smash into what was hidden there. Nothing responded to his tugging and pulling.

"I can't stop it!"

Elly Mae nodded. "Don't you feel it?" she asked.

Feel what? was Jim's first thought. Then he knew. They *were* being pulled on! It was not that thing which had called for help—this was different. It was not alive . . . it was. . . . No, he could not explain what was drawing them on. Only that it was frightening enough to make him shiver.

The mist was so heavy they could not see

49

beyond the edge of the boat's cockpit. It was thick and wet like a real rain. Elly Mae kept smearing her hand across her face, but she could not clear away the mist to see any better.

This place was even more frightening than the silent City. They knew a little about the City, but they knew absolutely nothing about this. Now that the force that had called to them was dead, Elly Mae was afraid. When it had called, she had wanted only to go and help. But now . . . She put out her hand to Jim and his fingers curled tightly about hers. Jim must feel the same way she did.

The boat slowed. Jim did not even try to run it now. The engine sputtered into silence, although they continued moving forward.

Soon there was something overhead. They passed under a roof of some kind and kept on going. The mist was thinner now. They could see dark walls around them. Those walls looked as if they were made of smoothed stone.

Elly Mae shivered. "Where is this place?" she asked in a quavery voice.

"I don't know. . ." Jim answered. "It's awful dark though."

Where were they heading? And what was pulling them now that the engine had stopped?

All at once there was light ahead. Very slowly the boat was swept on toward the light. It coasted through a wash of water into a narrow slit between two long, outward-stretching arms of stone. There it came to so sudden a stop that both children were jolted out of their seats.

There were other such slits on either side. Boats were in two of them. Both were empty. Jim looked at Elly Mae.

"We got here," he said. "Only where are we?"

"Inside the bubble—I think." she answered. She was looking around. "Only— there ain't anybody here. Where did—that *thing* go?"

Jim was relieved that nothing had come to meet them. They had found a way in under the bubble. Now maybe they had just better go back. He pulled at the starting controls, but there was no response.

"Hadn't we better look?" Elly Mae asked as she edged towards the wharf. "Maybe—maybe it ain't dead—just hurt bad . . . ."

She was sure that it was dead, but sitting and waiting for trouble was not the way Elly Mae lived. She always wanted to meet it. Sometimes you could even lick it if you went right ahead.

"Maybe . . ." Jim agreed reluctantly. Elly Mae was right that it would not do any good just to sit here. He wished he had a gun—though he did not know how to shoot one, or a big stick, or a stone he could throw—anything. He looked around the boat. Nothing . . .

"Come on, then!" Elly Mae was already scrambling onto the wharf. Jim followed. Ahead lay another tunnel. Unless one tried to swim out the way the boat had brought them, that dark hole was the only way out of here.

52

Neither of them was in a big hurry. They went slowly, looking carefully around, watching for anything that might be hiding. Cautiously they entered the tunnel. Once inside they saw above them lines that cast a pale glow downward, giving off enough light for them to see.

The tunnel led upwards. Then it levelled off. There was more light ahead, a stronger light. They hurried toward it.

They came out into a very large room, more like a cave. Most of the floor was covered with a pool which did not appear to be deep. The pool was divided by small low walls, their surface just above the lapping water.

The far end of the cavernous room showed another dark hole in the wall, a hole that was set low so that only a little of it showed above water. On the edge of the pool, not far from where they stood, something moved.

Elly Mae cried out. A creature which looked like both a spider and a crab—a big one—clicked wicked-looking claws as it

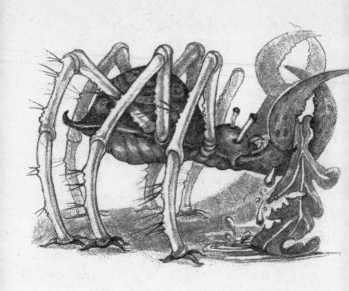

plopped into the water and went down one of the runways under water towards the hole in the far wall.

Where it had been there lay long strips of what looked like torn up leaves—green splotched with brown. There was a thick stem also, which had been broken, or cut, into several pieces from which there still oozed greenish liquid.

4

The Sea Garden

"WHAT IS it?" Elly Mae took one cautious step, then another, eyeing the thing lying on the stone.

"Some kind of plant—looks like." Jim was watching the spot where the clawed creature had plopped into the water. It had moved so fast. He did not like what he had seen of it.

Elly Mae squatted down to look closer at the torn leaves and broken stem.

"Looky here! See this . . ." She was pointing at the largest piece of leaf.

Jim, with one eye on the water, came closer. The leaf was spread flat on the stone and there were little balls along one edge that was torn the least. Before he could protest Elly Mae stretched out a finger to prod one of the balls. It rolled free across the stone and would have gone into the pool if Jim had not put out his foot to stop it.

He picked it up. It was heavy, about the size of a marble, and he was sure it was some kind of metal. But what was it doing caught in the leaf?

"There're more—see?" Elly Mae was picking up the balls, not only from the remains of the leaves, but a few which lay free on the stone. "What are they?"

Jim shook his head. "Don't know. Maybe we'd better leave them alone." But he did not drop the one he had picked up. This place was much stranger than the City. He could understand the City and the robots that patroled it. But this place was weird—a torn-up plant, and that crab—or whatever it was. What did it all mean?

Elly Mae, one hand clutched around the bits of metal that she had picked from the torn plant, stood up and looked around.

"What was this for?" she echoed Jim's silent question aloud. "Funny kind of place. What do you suppose *that* is?"

She pointed to the wall ahead of them. Set into the stone was a mesh of metal, like a window screen. Jim went to it. He could see nothing behind it, but a smooth and gleaming plate.

All at once Elly Mae shivered. "I don't like this place. Let's go back, Jim."

She edged away from the screened plate on the wall and headed towards the passage leading to the boat. But Jim sighted something else—a ruffling of the water in one of those troughs on the floor.

"Come on!" He grabbed Elly Mae's arm, hurried her toward the passage. "Something's down there . . ."

More than just one something, he was sure. Elly Mae took a step or two, then stopped short, holding back against his pull.

"Listen . . . !" she urged.

"To what?" Then Jim caught her meaning. This was not words forming in his

58

head as when the Ka'ats talked. This was more of a feeling.

Elly Mae stood very still, but her head turned so she could see the low opening at the far side where the water came washing in. She made an effort to think. Only it was not think-talk as she did with Mer.

"Who are you?" She both thought that and asked it aloud, as if the sound of her words was also important.

"Look!" Jim jerked at her arm, made her turn her head.

The mesh screen on the wall was no longer plain grey like the stone around it. Little sparks of light ran along its wires, making it glow like the insides of a heated toaster.

Jim dropped his hold on Elly Mae and moved closer to the screen, though not too close. The light that ran along the wires died. The mesh became dull and dead again.

"Who are you?" Jim echoed Elly's question.

Once more light ran from wire to wire. Elly Mae thought she understood.

"It ain't a think-thing. It's like the City machines—you talk to it!"

Once more the wires were dull. Jim stared at it.

"Doesn't answer to all talk," he said thoughtfully. "Now why . . . ?"

"Think and talk together, maybe," Elly Mae suggested. "That was what I was doin' when it came alive first."

"But the City people didn't think-talk," Jim said slowly.

Elly Mae looked away from the screen to the water. There was something coming. And—it wanted something, too. It was frightened, but it was coming on because what it wanted was important—it needed them!

"It wants us . . ." she said. "Don't you feel it?"

Jim nodded. "We'd better get away—it may be a trap!"

There was a change in the water along one of the walled runs, a splashing. Out of

60

the surface came the top of a plant. Leaves, which had been curled about its stem, spread wide as soon as they lifted into the air. The plant continued to move towards them.

It looked like the one that had been torn to pieces, but this was larger and it was moving as if it were an animal rather than a rooted plant.

Elly Mae knelt at the edge of the pool. The two top leaves of the thick stem turned their upper side to face her, as if they were watching eyes.

"It's afraid!" Elly Mae said softly. "It has come but it is afraid!"

Jim felt the fear, too. This was the same fear that had frightened him during their flight over the domed island. But plants couldn't feel or think! What was it?

The leafed top drew closer. It rose higher above the water. If it had been out on the ledge, it would have stood taller than either of them.

Now Elly Mae could see round, cord-like things growing out of the stem below its

61

wider and larger leaves. These uncoiled and reached out to fasten on the walls under the water. Once secure, they grew tight, and with them the plant pulled itself forward.

There was nothing scary about the plant itself. What was scary was knowing that it knew they were there. And that it had come to meet them!

A clicking sound startled both children. They looked around wildly. The screen was alight again but the light came in patterns, some wires black, others lighted.

"The plant—it's trying to talk!" Elly Mae waved to the screen. "It's trying to talk to us—that way."

"Only we can't understand it," Jim listened to the clicking sounds and watched the plant. It swayed back and forth, waving the leaves below the uppermost two which were still fixed and steady and turned forward in a way he could only think of as eyes.

The lower leaves had the balls of metal stuck in them, showing bright as it moved, even in this dull light.

"It's afraid . . ." Elly Mae slipped down until her feet hung just above the water, leaning forward in her eagerness to understand. "It's just awfully afraid! But not of us . . ."

Jim caught that, too. The crab things . . . ! Even as he thought of the one he had seen he had seen slip into the water earlier, the plant shuddered. Its leaves waved more wildly. Its pull on the cords which it used to draw itself on grew faster. If a plant could be said to run, this one was certainly trying to do so.

Elly Mae drew back, for the thin cords were clamping down on the stone very close to the rim of the pool. As she gave it room, the cords fell on the very spot where she had been sitting, grew taught as the thick stem sloped forward.

With great effort the plant pulled the forepart of its body up on the shelf. More of it still trailed back into the water and Jim guessed that the root remained there.

Now it brought its leaves together, scraped the surfaces against one another. Loosened from small pockets which contained them, the balls of metal, large and small, fell to the rock surface. When it had shed all that it carried, it squatted lower, apparently awaiting something in return.

"It wants us to have 'em . . ." Elly Mae was sweeping the balls of metal together. "It brought them for us . . ."

Jim was sure she was right. But it was hard to believe that a walking, thinking plant provided the metal for the People. Was this the way they *mined*? Did the plants go underwater and dig? He shook his head. If they could only find a book or a tape or *something* which would explain.

"I wish we could really talk . . ." Elly Mae faced the plant and spoke slowly.

The chattering on the wire screen grew a fraction louder. Now the plant swayed, its leaves rising and falling. Elly Mae looked over her shoulder to Jim.

"It wants something—something important! And I don't know what! I just gotta learn!" She dropped the metal nuggets and rolled her fingers into fists. "We gotta learn, Jim. It's important! Maybe Mer can."

Her head lifted a little and there was a closed look on her face. Jim knew she was trying to think-talk with the Ka'at. Would the distance between the island and the shore be too great? He ought to try Tiro, too. After all, this was the Ka'ats' own world, and if anyone knew about water plants that produced metal—they ought to.

Jim closed his eyes and sharpened his

thought. He pictured Tiro and then think-talked.

"Yes, cubling? What have you found?"

The answer came faintly but Jim was relieved. They were not cut off from the shore. He tried to shape his answer as clearly as he could—the coming to this cave pool—the plant that had appeared with a gift of metal.

Tiro's answer was quick and sure: "This is a thing of importance, kin-cub. Can you turn off that force which keeps us away from the island? We must see for ourselves . . ."

Turn off the force? Perhaps they could, just as he and Elly Mae had turned off the power in the city. He sent that message and opened his eyes—just in time.

"Look out! Jim, get them—stop them!" Elly Mae's voice rose to a scream. The plant was threshing back and forth wildly. He could feel the fear and pain it broadcast. There was movement in the water. The crabs were back! They were attacking the plants' roots.

Jim looked about wildly for a weapon. If he had even a club! The plant was twitching, and Elly Mae had reached out her hands to it. Those green cords which had drawn it to them snapped out, fastened on the girl's arms and hands. She pulled back and the plant followed her farther and farther out of the water. A thick root was exposed. To the bits of it which projected on either side clung the crabs, slashing.

Jim crouched past Elly Mae and the struggling plant to kick out at the crabs. He shouted as he beat at them. They dropped off one by one as the plant came farther out of the water. But some were struggling to get up onto the rim of the pool. Jim kicked again. There was a sharp pain, one of the crabs had turned on him and pinched with its claws right through the boot on his foot. He stamped down and then kicked.

Elly Mae was screaming. And her voice was picked up in some strange fashion so that the sound filled the whole cavern. More of the crabs dropped away. Jim knew

it was not his efforts that made them go. The noise? Did Elly Mae's screams make them afraid?

He added his voice to hers. The noise was such that it made his ears hurt. But the crabs were going. The plant had toppled forward holding on to Elly Mae, its two-leafed top well above her head.

"Yaaaah!" Elly Mae was not screaming now, she was yelling. Like Jim, she had guessed about the sound, too. "Yaaaah!" Her throat almost hurt as she got that cry out.

The clawed creatures were going. Ripples sped away from where they had attacked the plant. Jim kept up his shouts until he was sure they had retreated.

"They ain't going to get you!!" Elly Mae's voice sounded a bit hoarse. She was speaking directly to the plant, which now was slowly straightening up its main stem. But the cords from beneath its leaves still tightly clasped the girl.

"They're gone—for now," Jim said, but he kept a wary eye on the water. He did not believe that the crabs could be so easily defeated even though they did not like noise.

Then he felt it. Just as the noise had seemed to deafen him when they had both yelled together, so did this sound shake his whole body. It was as if they were all caught in a huge cage that shook from side to side. He even put out his hands to try to keep his balance.

The plant loosed its hold on Elly Mae. Its root slid back into the water. They could no longer feel its fear. Rather there was another feeling—a good feeling—as if there was nothing to be afraid of now.

The rolling sensation continued, but they really were not rolling at all! It just seemed that way, the sensation spreading up into their bodies through their feet. Jim shut his eyes. He felt as if he was being tipped from one side to the other, just as if he were in a boat.

"What . . . what. . . ." he heard Elly Mae ask, and opened his eyes.

Hers were very big and she was looking at him in surprise.

70

"It's all shaky—everything is shaky."

Jim made another guess. "No, we just feel that way. It's a vibration in this." He stamped one foot against the rock.

Already the sensation was lessening. The plant had settled on the ledge, letting its root trail into the water. It no longer broadcast feelings of fear or of danger. Whatever had happened, they had driven away the crabs, at least for the moment. But they would have to do something before they came back.

Elly Mae was thinking. "We want Mer," she said firmly, "Mer and Tiro, and maybe Micha. We have to find a way to get them here. Mer told me so."

"Tiro did, too. We've got to see what we can do. But what about—about that? If we leave it here, the crabs will come again." He pointed to the plant.

"It isn't afraid now. Maybe the crabs won't come soon. And we'll hurry. . . ." Elly Mae was already on her way to the tunnel.

71

5

The Secret of the Dome

THE BOAT was where they had left it. Behind them was the tunnel that led to the sea garden in which the plant had traveled, but—where did they go from here? Though neither Jim nor Elly Mae could see another opening, they were sure there must be another way out of the cave.

Slowly they went along the wall. Elly Mae was thinking hard—there must be a way. But she saw no signs of another opening.

Jim stopped short. His head turned slowly from left to right as he studied the firm wall. Elly Mae was running her fingers along its damp surface.

"There's just gotta be a way out!"

"Sure. But where?"

Elly Mae's eyes closed suddenly. The People of the City did not use the think-talk of the Ka'ats—they had feared and hated that. They used buttons, and levers—and—sound! Sounds made the machines back in the city work. That wire screen had come to life when they had thought and talked together. She ran her tongue over her lower lip.

"Maybe we gotta make sounds," she said slowly.

Jim laughed. "Like Ali Baba?"

Elly Mae turned her head to look at him. "Who's that?"

"A guy in a fairy tale. He found this cave full of things robbers had hidden. But the door would only open if you said 'Open sesame.' He hid and heard one of the robbers say it and then got in himself. Only what are we going to say here? We couldn't find the right words in a million-trillion years!"

To his surprise Elly Mae looked back to the wall and said gravely, "Open sesame!"

"Hey, that's just a story!" Jim protested. "It won't work here."

She shrugged. "Maybe not. No harm tryin'. But I'll bet there *is* something that will. We just gotta keep tryin'."

"We could try and try and never find the right words. We don't know how the People spoke."

Elly Mae remained stubbornly set before the wall. "We can jus' try," she repeated. And she began the crooning gibberish she had used to set machines in the city going.

The wall remained as it was, without any signs of a break on its surface.

"It's no use, I tell you!" Jim exploded. "We're never going to hit on the right sound. Yaaaaah!" To show her he turned and yelled at the wall with all the force of his lungs.

"Look!"

What a moment before had looked to be solid stone now showed the dark line of a crack.

74

"Do that again!" commanded Elly Mae.

Surprised at what he saw, Jim drew a deep breath and let loose another shout. Nothing happened.

"Told you so . . ."

"You jus' didn't get it right," she answered. "Do it again—try to make it sound different."

Jim could not remember now how the first shout had sounded. But he let loose a third shout.

"See!" Elly Mae danced from one foot to another.

The crack widened. Now it made a very narrow door through which they might even squeeze if they would go sidewise and push a lot. But to go in there. . . ! Jim thought of that crack closing again, the way the doors in the City would slide shut if not wedged open. He did not want to be crushed by the wall shutting when he was half through.

He ran back to the boats. There was nothing in the one in which they had come that he could use for a wedge. In a big box in the other was a pile of the metal balls such as the plant had given them. He scooped these up with both hands. But they rolled easily. The door could swing them aside and close. No matter how high he might pile them, they would not work.

Elly Mae had caught the idea in his mind. Though they did not truly think-talk to one another as they did with the Ka'ats, it often seemed that something plain in one mind could be picked up by the other. She had gone to the boat and was pulling at the padded cushion on the seat.

It came loose at her jerking and she brought it over to where Jim had found the balls. Together they were able to tear open a corner of the covering (it must have been well-rotted in the years it had been in the boat) and fill it with the balls of metal. They now had a heavy block of metal-enforced cushion, enough to keep the wall door open.

When they had wedged it into place, Jim squeezed through first. It was dark beyond, but much wider, once you were on the other side of the door. He reached back and caught Elly Mae's hand.

Still clasping hands, they reached out with their other fingers and located walls on either side. Running their finger tips along the walls, they went forward slowly, often looking back at the narrow patch of light that marked the door.

"Ughhh!" Elly Mae let out a gasp as she stumbled forward, letting go her hold on Jim. "There's stairs here—going up. Gotta feel the steps."

They crawled up the stairs on their hands and knees, feeling, as Elly Mae had said, for the next one above. Then, at last, they found a place where there were no more stairs. Jim got to his feet cautiously and hunted for the wall with one hand. He slid forward one step, then two. . . .

There was a sound like something scraping. Before them opened another door which they had made no sound to summon, and light streamed out.

"Come on!" Jim caught at Elly Mae and urged her forward into the light. Maybe he ought to be more careful about what lay ahead, but, having made that journey in the dark, he wanted to be where he could see again.

They had come into a big room which had box-like machines like those of the City all around the sides. Jim was sure that these probably worked the same way. In the very center of the room, under a cluster of lights hanging from the roof, stood a flat-surfaced block that might have been used as a desk. On it was a pile of square objects a little larger than Jim's hand.

Each square had colored strips across one end, and each color was stacked together—green, yellow, blue, and two red, and a single black. Behind the desk was a wide chair, big enough to hold maybe three or four Jims and Elly Maes.

The walls were transparent and looked out into the steamy mist that surrounded the bubble.

"Sure is big!" Elly Mae looked from one side to the other. "How are we gonna find the thing to shut off? This ain't like the City at all."

In the City they had been helped by an energy globe taken from a flyer. It had led them straight to the main power source. There Elly Mae had simply, though courageously, smashed the larger globe, turning off the energy by which the city and the robots operated. Here there was no globe of fire nor anything else to point out what they must attack.

"That. . ." Jim pointed to the desk,

"must be where they sat—the people who ran everything."

"Don't look like any machine to me," Elly Mae answered doubtfully.

"Not a machine," Jim said. "Just the place where they could see if all these were going all right . . ." He waved a hand at the boxes along the glass walls.

The huge room was very silent. They could see every bit of it and there were no moving robots here. Still Jim did not like going farther in. If this was a place important to the People—and it must be—then there could well be traps they could not even imagine—until they were caught.

"I'll go down that side," Elly Mae waved to the left, "and you go down this. Do we see anything we just yell out . . . right?"

"We don't even know what to look for," Jim said slowly. But he was already starting down his side of the domed room.

Most of the boxes were alike. He thought maybe they were computers of some sort. But they must all be shut down. Elly Mae's voice reached him as she tried talking, singing, or yelling at one after the other. Suddenly Jim gave up and went directly to the desk in the center. This, he was very sure, was the important place.

He turned over the squares with the colored ends. They were plain gray except for those bands of color. At first he thought they might be small boxes. But he could see no lines around their edges to show they could be opened.

Before the middle position in the long seat there was a slit in the table edge which he only saw when he got close. On a guess he picked up one of the squares and measured it against the hole. It was an exact fit. These squares were meant to go in there. Suppose he fitted the square into the hole—then what would happen? He wiped his hands down the front of his furry suit. They felt wet. Suppose he chose a wrong one and something blew up, or a robot would come in after them, or he and Elly Mae would be caught in a cage like the Ka'ats had been when they got into the old city?

"What you doin' there?" Elly Mae came back from her useless trip of trying to awaken the machines.

"It's these things," Jim pointed to the narrow blocks. "See this hole? They were made to go in there."

"What for, I wonder? Why not just put one in . . ." Elly Mae reached out toward the pile of blocks but Jim hurriedly pushed it away.

"We don't know what will happen."

"Well, unless we try it we ain't never going to find out. How do we even know we can get away from here? Maybe that boat ain't going to run the other way. Did you think of that?"

Jim had thought of it and pushed the thought to the back of his mind. It was one he didn't want to remember.

"We can ask Mer. . ." Elly Mae had her eyes closed, that odd look on her face that meant she was thought-sending to her Ka'at kin on the shore.

Mer might not know, but what about Tiro? Tiro was older than Mer and had been a scout much longer. Jim summoned into his mind the image of the big black and white Ka'at who was his close friend.

"What have you found?" Tiro's think-talk came clearly.

Jim tried to picture as carefully as he could the big room, but mainly the desk with its slit and the waiting squares which could be fitted into it. He was not sure that Tiro could give him any help. Though the Ka'ats ran many of the machines that they had adapted from those they had taken from the People, they did not understand the machines in the City, nor probably those here.

"I will tell this to Micha who has come to join us," came Tiro's message. "He knows more of the People's machines than I."

Jim sat down on the bench and a moment later Elly Mae joined him.

"Mer didn't know," she reported. "She's going to ask Micha."

"That's what Tiro said, too."

"Seems like," Elly Mae leaned over and gathered the squares to lay them out in a row, "these here colors ought to mean something important." She separated a red and a green one and put them down side by side. "Now that there—back home, that meant you can walk—" she pushed the green one a little with her forefinger, "and then this you can't walk—cross the street." Now she tapped the red one.

"Red for danger—that's what it meant," Jim nodded. "And black," he pointed to the single square marked with that color, "that could be bad, too. But we can't be sure, Elly Mae. Maybe on this world they thought green bad and red good."

"What's this . . . ?" Elly Mae leaned farther out across the desk. She was using her forefinger like a pencil drawing a line and now Jim saw what she was doing.

There was a much larger square there, part of the surface of the desk. It was the very same color so it was hard to see unless, as Elly Mae was doing, you traced the edge around the four sides. When he slid his finger across the part enclosed by those faint lines, he felt a substance which was very smooth—like glass.

Elly Mae had been trying to fit her fingernails into the crack.

"Don't seem as if it's a lid," she said. Now she pushed down on it with her whole palm. "Can't lift it, nor push it neither."

The slit they had noticed first lay immediately below the mysterious, almost hidden, square. A sudden thought struck Jim. What if it was a picture screen—like those on the sides of the machines in the city? And just maybe, if you put in one of the squares, it would work!

Without stopping to wait for any word from Micha, thought-sent by Tiro, he caught at the nearest square, one of the green ones, and fitted it into the slit. It would not go all the way, only about a third of it went in. He was afraid to try and force it deeper.

But . . .

The square in the table top changed!

There was a flickering at first, then they could see plainly.

"It's where that big old plant is!" Elly Mae cried out.

True enough. Only this view was from the top, as if they could see straight through the ceiling of that cave. The plant was still there, though it had settled farther back into the water, and those two leaves which had seemed to be its eyes were turned around, facing the opening through which it had come.

But that was not all. They not only saw the plant—now they could hear. The sound was loud as if the plant itself were shouting—just as the children had shouted to drive off the crab things. But this was not a shout—it was more like music. The plant was beginning to weave its stem back and forth in a strange way, keeping time to the music.

There was a change in the water, too. It looked brown, as if someone had spilled a big coffee pot into it.

"What's happening . . . ?" Elly Mae asked.

Jim could have echoed her. There was agitation in the water by the sea entrance. The leaf tip of another plant showed above the surface, a second already crowding in behind that.

"We—this . . ." Jim slapped his hand down on the table, "must be calling those things. . . ."

6

The Attack from the Sea

"Turn it off!" Elly Mae grabbed at the block and pulled it out of the slit before Jim could move.

"What did you do that for?" the boy demanded.

"Didn't you see them? Those crab things? They was comin', too!"

Jim had not seen anything but the plants. But Elly Mae could be right—anything could happen in this place.

"They'll get the plant things," Elly Mae continued. "We gotta do something and do it quick!"

"What?" Jim wanted to know. "Go back down there and yell at them again?"

"If we have to. . . ."

But he wanted to be sure. Elly Mae held on to the green banded square and he could not pull it away from her. But there was another which looked just the same. Jim caught that up and shoved it down in the slit.

Once more a picture, just like the TV back on their own world, formed on the desk screen. Only now they did not see the walled pool where the plants came. Instead they were watching the edge of the sea itself, as if they were standing outside the bubble on the island.

Again there was a sound. This time a shrill hooting which hurt the ears. The waves washed the sand and rock and now there was movement through those waves. But the children could not be quite sure what caused it. For whatever was causing that disturbance did not rise above the surface.

"Take it out!" Elly Mae dropped the square she was holding and reached for the new one.

Jim pushed her away. "Let it alone . . ."

"You want the crab things to get them?" she demanded. "Don't you feel it—right in your head? They don't make think-talk but they feel!"

He shivered. She was right. That fear was back. Quickly he snatched loose the second square. What did it all mean?

"We called them," Elly Mae threw the square with such force that it slid over the other side of the desk and fell to the floor. "Don't you see? We called them, and now the crab things are going to eat them. We did it!" She was close to tears.

Jim knew she was right. The plants had been answering a call which the People must have set. They had come and now the crabs would get them! How could they be stopped?

"Try that," Elly Mae took up a red banded square. "Just maybe that will send them away again."

Hoping she was right, Jim fitted the square into the slot. The mirror plate came to life, but what they saw now was neither the pool underground, nor the beach of the island. Rather they found themselves looking straight at Micha and Tiro who were pacing up and down in one of the buildings ashore.

"Tiro! Jim nearly shouted. He saw the big Ka'at whirl about, ears flattened to his skull, hair rising to ridge his spine, his eyes slitted.

"Tiro," hurriedly Jim switched to thought-talk. "I can see you! Can you see me?"

Both the Ka'ats were looking in his direction, but they seemed puzzled. Then Tiro's answer came:

"We see only the wall of this place, yet your voice came out of it. This is more of the People's learning. . . ."

It gave Jim confidence that he could see Tiro even if the Ka'at could not view him. And, as fast as he could, he thought-talked about what had happened during the last few minutes.

"We must come," Tiro had conferred nose to nose with Micha, now he thought-sent strongly. "Can you find us a way?"

Jim looked at the squares. Maybe one of them was the key to the opening of the island for the Ka'ats. But dare he try them one after another without being sure that he would not trigger a weapon? There was really nothing to do but chance it.

"We'll try," he told Tiro. He pulled out the red-banded square and the picture of the building ashore was gone. Green was for the plants, the first red one had been to connect island to shore, maybe so orders could be passed. He had now some yellows and the one black. His hand hovered between one of the yellow and the black one.

"Try that," Elly Mae pointed to the black.

"I don't know," Jim was cautious. "Maybe black means something bad . . . ."

"Maybe so, maybe not." Elly Mae answered slowly. "It's the only one like that. Try it first. . . ."

"Here goes." Jim fitted the square in very fast. If he waited any longer he might not do it at all.

Nothing appeared on the screen, as if the new square did not work. Then Elly Mae let out a squeak of surprise and pointed at the curve of the wall. The steamy clouds which formed a curtain outside were coming apart. That mist was drifting or being blown away by a sea wind. They could see well beyond now.

The children hurried to press their faces to the rounded, transparent wall. From here they could even see the shore and the buildings where the boats had been. But if the clouding mist had gone, had the invisible guard against the Ka'ats also been shut off?

"Looky there!" Elly Mae saw the landing place first. It was not raised as high as the room in which they stood but they could look down. It was broad and flat, and formed of the same grey material that covered the buildings and made up most of the machines of the people.

"Mer—we have to tell Mer!" She was already reaching out with think-talk, seeking Mer with the news that there was a place where a flyer might land.

Mer was quick to catch her message.

"They're going to try to come!" Elly Mae reported. "I knew we could do it! I just knew we could find the turn-off thing!"

"Maybe we did something else . . ." Jim had caught sight of what was happening down on the shore beyond the landing place and he shivered.

Crabs! Not just one or two—or a few as they had seen in the pool. The shore was crawling with them. There must be hundreds! And they were coming closer and closer to the bubble wall. He did not think they could break through, but some had already appeared at the edge of the landing place. And perhaps—he remembered that opening on the sea down in the pool—they *could* get in there!

Elly Mae's eyes grew large. "Jim, what are we goin' to do? Mer and Tiro and Micha—those crab things will get them! We've got to do something!"

Jim could see no door in this dome room,

nothing to give them a chance to reach the landing place from here. But there must be an opening somewhere! The People had come both by sea and by air, of that he was now sure. So—how did they get in from outside?

Meanwhile, he must warn Tiro. He sent a hurried think-call.

"We have seen those you speak of," Tiro replied. "They are eaters of meat as well as plants, and many together are a danger. We shall have to think about coming. . . ."

Jim caught at Elly Mae's arm.

"We did what we came for," he said. "Now let's go back . . . ."

"We can't! They—they're getting the plant people! Oh!" Her hands went to her ears. But she could not shut out of her mind the pain and terror of the strange sea dwellers who had been caught in that underground place and had no defense against the death which clawed at them now.

Jim bit his lip. He did not see how they could help the plants. But they had to, he knew that. If it had not been for his putting in the caller, there might not be any plants to suffer. So he really was the one responsible. But all those crabs. . . . He and Elly Mae could not hope to fight off hundreds!

"Come back!" Tiro's voice broke into his mind in a sharp order.

"I can't, not yet," Jim answered. No, not until he was sure there was nothing he could do. But Elly Mae could and must. He did not want to see her surrounded somewhere in this place by waves of crabs. They were on the move outside. Lines of them were now halfway across the landing place.

"Elly Mae," he said, "you got to take the boat and get away. . . ."

She was shaking her head firmly before he said the word "boat."

"Ain't gonna do it! Them crabs ain't gonna let me neither! Who says they can't crawl right outta' the water and into the boat?"

She was right. Jim swallowed. To go out in a boat might be very dangerous. He did not know much about crabs—even the crabs of his own world. Those here on the Star Ka'at's world might be even worse to face. He was sure, even at this distance, way above the landing stage, that some of those gathering below were much larger than those he and Elly Mae had chased away in the room where the pool was.

Now the fear of the plants, which he could feel in his mind, was terrible. Like Elly Mae, he wished that putting his hands over his ears could keep it out of his head.

Elly Mae started towards the door through which they had come.

"We've gotta go and help, we just gotta!" she cried.

Jim had not had a chance to stop her, he could only follow. But to head down into the darkness toward those crabs made him a little sick. Now the silent screams of the plants roared in his head.

Elly Mae tried not to think. If she did, she was sure she would stop right where she was. But there was no sense in just waiting around for those nasty crab things to come and get her. She and Jim had to yell at them—hard—just like they did before. She drew a deep breath and then another getting ready to give such a yell as soon as she was able to see one of them coming, clicking its big claws at her.

If they could only help the plant people! She did not realize that she was crying as she dropped from one step to the next, though her throat felt scratchy now.

They squeezed through the propped-open door. Jim tugged at the weighted cushion bag. No use leaving that doorway open for any crabs to go marching up. He looked around quickly. The boats still were floating quietly in the water, and there was no sign of the crabs.

Elly Mae stooped and caught at the edge of the heavy cushion bag.

She had a hard time lifting it, but maybe this could squash some of those old crabs.

"What you trying to do?"

She did not look at Jim. She had barely heard him. Those plant people made her feel so very bad.

"Gonna smash them crabs," she said, jerking the bag along, "gonna smash 'em right down dead!"

Jim grabbed at the other end of the bag. Between them they were able to carry it.

"We gotta yell, too," Elly Mae reminded him.

"Sure."

It was as if they had both drawn in a deep breath together and loosed it again in one big shout. The noise spread ahead of them down the passage. Again they yelled as they hurried ahead as fast as they could.

Elly Mae shivered. One of the plant-people must have just died. Its dying hurt in her head. They had better hurry or there would not be any left.

As Jim and Elly Mae came into the pool room they saw the crabs tearing at two dead plants, shredding leaves from the stems and breaking the stems in their huge claws. Two more of the plant things had climbed nearly out of the water. They were striking out at the crabs with those vines they had used to draw themselves along. But they could not beat off the enemy.

Once more the children yelled. This time the wire screen blazed up high while their shouts resounded louder and louder.

The crabs, busy at tearing the dead plants, drew back. Those attacking the still-living ones stopped their claw-clicking advance. A second yell sent the outer fringe of the crabs scuttling toward the pool. Jim noticed that they did not jump in and swim. Instead they sank. He could not see what happened then, for that brown stain hid everything below the surface.

"Again!" Jim panted.

A third time they shouted together. The plants out of the water swayed back and forth as if those sounds were like a wind blowing them. More of the crabs plopped down into the pool, but not all of them retreated.

Though they no longer tore at the living

plants, a number of crabs encircled them, refusing to be frightened away. Jim dropped his end of the heavy bag and ran towards those closest to the edge of the pool.

His feet skidded on one of the leaves which had been torn from a dead plant. He yelled, this time in fear, as he slipped toward the dark water. There was nothing to hold on to—he was going right in on top of the crabs!

Then—something whipped out of the air, closed in a tight ring around the wrist of one outflung arm. It caught and held. He did not quite go over the edge. The plant, which had thrown one of its largest and thickest vines to catch at him, was pulled over by his weight until the double leaves of its head nearly touched his face.

In that moment, when he was close to it, he could see the odd veining on those leaves, lines which did indeed seem to outline the shape of eyes.

Elly Mae was beside him now, catching at his other arm, jerking him back from the pool. The crabs, which had circled the plants, were moving at them. Before he had risen from his knees, Jim yelled once more. This time the fear of what had nearly happened made his cry even stronger. Back tumbled the crabs into the murky water.

The crabs were going, but Jim had a feeling they had not retreated very far. The plant had loosened its hold on his wrist and snapped back to stand upright. It had saved him, that was for sure. And it was different from any plant he ever knew. It was, as Elly Mae had called it, a plant person. They could not just leave a person, one who had saved him, here to be killed by the crabs. There must be a way. But he and Elly Mae could not go on screaming for very long. If there was just another sound—one which they could keep on broadcasting for awhile. . . . If they only knew more about the things the People had left behind! Jim was sure that somewhere there must be a way of really fighting the crabs. Maybe they could find it.

7

The Great Shout

ELLY MAE looked at Jim. "What're we gonna do? We just can't keep on yelling like that forever—"

"I know," he agreed. His throat already hurt. And those crabs which had fallen back in the water—would they tear up the roots of the plants which still reached down under the clouded surface?

"Where are we gonna get a noise?" Elly Mae went over to look at the wire netting which always lit up when they yelled and which seemed to make the sound louder and last longer. "We gotta learn how to run this thing here. . . ."

But how? Its use was another of the secrets of the People. Jim wanted to kick that screen—make it work. This was like trying to read a book in which all the words were printed in another language. He rubbed his throat. If they were back on their own world, they could have a sound tape made of their yelling and just keep playing the tape. Maybe the People had things like sound tapes, too. Or—for a moment he was startled—what about the Ka'ats?

Most of their machines (in fact all Jim had seem them use) were run by thinking at them. The People's had run by sound, apparently sounds not unlike what Jim and Elly Mae themselves made. Hand and sound, the People used both. Judging from the old stories of the Ka'ats, the People had been so afraid of think-talk that they had destroyed much of the surface of their own world to wipe out all the Ka'ats, once they learned that the Ka'ats could speak by thought.

But the Ka'ats did make sounds, too. They could purr, and they had other sounds—some very loud and queer (to Jim and Elly Mae at least). For other Ka'ats those sounds had meanings. If People machines would not run to the Ka'at sounds, that did not mean they might not be used in another way.

"Ka'ats can make noises. . . ." Jim was still trying to work out an idea.

"They sure can!" Elly Mae agreed. "You think . . ." she glanced from Jim to the netting on the wall and back again, "you think," she began again, "that maybe Mer, and Tiro could come out here and yell and scare off the crabs? Maybe even better than us?"

"Could be . . . ."

"Then we got to tell them!" Elly Mae said promptly. She closed her eyes as she did most times when she was think-talking. Somehow it made it much easier to see Mer inside her mind.

And Mer was there, just as Elly Mae hoped she would be. The girl tried to explain and Mer grew quite excited.

"We have captured one of the pincher ones," Mer answered. "We shall try on it what you have said. Let us see . . ." Her think-talk faded and Elly Mae spoke to Jim.

"They got them one of these here crabs and they're gonna try yelling at it their ownselves. Maybe that will work."

Jim sat down on the rock of the pool edge. The plant which had saved him was drooping a little, its leaves not held straight out, but falling closer to its heavy stem. He no longer felt its fear, but rather that it was very tired.

There were more metal balls lying among the dead plants. And the living one had shed others which lay in a half circle around it. Where did they get that metal? How could plants mine for it? You had to have picks and shovels to dig. Jim tried to remember what little he knew of mines and miners on his own world. He had seen pictures of coal miners riding down into the ground to work. But they were in places on shore, not in the water. And a plant could not carry a shovel nor dig holes. . . .

He was trying to solve that puzzle when Tiro's voice rang into his head:

"The kin-cubling was right! These with claws can be made afraid by our cries. We are coming to you. . . ."

Jim stood up. "They're going to come out. . . ."

Elly Mae nodded. I know. We gotta find the way outta here. Only—if we leave the plant those crabs may come back."

She was right. But it was also true that if the Ka'ats came in on the landing place they might not be able to find a way into the bubble shelter.

"I'm going to find them a way." Elly Mae started back to the tunnel mouth. "You just gotta stay here and yell at the crabs."

"I'll go. . . ."

But Elly Mae was already at the tunnel. "You can yell louder—and maybe longer. Let me try any way. If I can't find any door, I'll come back and let you try."

She hurried down the tunnel. Where was she going to look for any door? Jim had found the other one which took them up

108

into the bubble. But that was above the level of the landing place. A door to that ought to be farther down.

Back in the place where the boats were docked Elly Mae started to search along the wall again. It must be farther along than where the other opening was, more to the other end of this cave place. So it was there that she moved close to the stone and ran her hands along it.

This rock did not feel any different and she was almost to the end of where she could walk. The rest was all water. She did not believe that the People would have a door which opened right into the water.

Yelling opened that other door—Jim's yelling. Could she now shout another one open? Elly Mae moved back a little to face the wall. Drawing in a deep breath she yelled with all her strength.

There was no opening. She rubbed the back of her hand across her mouth.

So her yell did not work. Maybe Jim would have to come and try. But not yet. She tried to think carefully. If a big, loud sound did not make it open—how about another kind of noise?

She remembered what Jim had said about the man in the story who had opened a cave by just saying the right kind of words. Only she did not know any words the People might have used. So. . . . Elly Mae shook her head. She was not going to give up yet. She ran her tongue across her lips and began:

"One, two three, O'Leary,
Four, five six, O'Leary,
Seven, eight, nine O'Leary,
Ten, O'Leary, postman out."

Elly Mae sang the old jump-rope ditty in her everyday voice, then a little louder. There was no answer. All right—so that did not work. But she had used that with one machine back in the city and it had. So some of her words must sound like those the People had used. Elly Mae sighed—if she only just *knew!*

"O'Leary, O'Leary, O'. . . ."

She had found it! There was a crack in

the rock, there really was! Elly Mae fairly danced she was so excited.

"O'Leary! O'Leary!"

A door—a real door! She must see it kept open. Elly Mae darted back and grabbed another of those tough cushions—but she did not stop to fill it with any of the metal. Instead she crammed it doubled up into the half open door as quickly as she could and then went through.

This place was not dark like the stairway passage. Instead there was light ahead. Just a few moments later she was out in the open, standing on the edge of the landing place.

Crabs—hundreds and hundreds—crawling back and forth like they were hunting something. Maybe just hunting her!

Elly Mae backed halfway into the passage. None was heading for her yet. And when they did she could yell—she could just yell hard enough to nearly bust her voice box.

There was another sound and she looked

skyward. It was the flyer! Elly Mae danced up and down in impatience. She and Jim had turned off all those clouds, but was there still a Ka'at warn-off so that Mer, Tiro and Micha could not land?

No, the flyer was coming down, straight down. And the crabs were not getting out of its way either. Elly Mae let out her loudest yell. The crabs turned in her direction. Some were backing away. She yelled again daring to move out now, intent upon getting the crabs off the landing place.

The flyer had not set down yet. It was hovering over the crabs. Now the bubble top lifted. Elly Mae saw not only Tiro, Mer, and Micha, but now there was Ana and two other of the chief Ka'ats. With their heads over the edge of the flyer's seat pit, all of them opened their mouths. The sounds which came out made even Elly Mae stumble back toward the tunnel, her hands going up to her ears.

They were screeching louder and worse than any Earth cat Elly Mae had ever heard in her life. And that sound! She watched the crabs scuttle to the edge of

the platform, drop over and away like sea-waves falling back from the shore.

It wasn't just one screech either. The flyer landed and the Ka'ats jumped out, not to join Elly Mae, but rather to march in a line to the side of the platform, uttering their terrible howls. The crabs were now all off the landing and hurrying away into the sea.

For a time as long as Elly Mae could count to maybe twenty, the Ka'ats remained in a line at the edge of the platform, giving those frightening cries. Then they stopped and, with Ana at the head, padded across to where Elly Mae stood.

"Ka'at kin," Ana thought, "this has been a good thing. Though what you have found is a greater puzzle than the city. Let us see . . . ."

"Please," Elly Mae dared to interrupt, even though she was just a little afraid of Ana. "Jim, he's down there with one of the plant people; and there's a lot more of those crabs . . . ."

"So? Let us go then." Ana was already

114

through the door, Elly Mae and the other Ka'ats behind her.

They hurried back through the place where the boats were and down the tunnel. Already they could hear Jim yelling. The crabs! Elly Mae began to run. But Tiro, Ana, and Mer kept pace at her side.

Now they were out in the pool cave. Jim stood before the plant, swinging the weighted cushion and yelling hoarsely. Out of the water crabs were crawling, heading straight for him.

The Ka'ats moved fast, coming together in a line and moving down upon the crabs. From them sounded a terrible shriek, as they cried out all together. Elly Mae screamed; for the wire screen on the wall blazed up in a great burst of fire and the noise was more than her ears could bear. She tried to plug them with her fingers.

Jim dropped the cushion and was covering his ears also. While the plant shook back and forth as if someone had hold of its stem and was shaking it hard. But the crabs—they did more than scuttle away this time. It was as if that awful sound simply swept them back into the water.

The Ka'ats lined up again as they had outside on the edge of the pool, their heads bent as if they could see down to the bottom in spite of the thick stain coloring the water. Elly Mae seeing that their mouths were closed, dared to take her fingers out of her ears.

Now she could not hear anything. Mer turned around and came trotting back to stand before her.

"The People who made this," the Ka'at thought, "made also that thing to increase sounds." She raised a paw and pointed to the wire screen from which the fire was now fading. "It is another of their secrets we cannot understand."

Ana, Micha, and one of the other Ka'ats, whom Elly Mae now saw was the great, golden Ka'at Fledyi, a leader of equal rank with Ana, had gone to stand before Jim. He stepped back out of the way so that the Ka'at now faced the plant.

Since the noise had stopped, the plant no

longer shook. Its head leaves came a little forward, as if it were looking down at the Ka'ats. Maybe it was surprised to see them. But Elly Mae knew that it was no longer afraid. Then words came into her mind again: "This—this life form cannot accept thought-send . . ." That was Ana. "Are you sure that it is more than just a plant?"

"It saved my life!" Jim thought that quickly, and went on to make a mind picture of how the plant had kept him from sliding into the pool.

"But it does not think," the Ka'at objected. "It does not understand us . . ."

"Maybe it's like the People in a way," the boy answered her. "They did not think-talk. The plant may not think in our way at all. But it did come when it was called, and it brought the metal." He pointed to the balls on the stone.

Micha leaned well over the edge of the pool, dipped his paw into the water and raised it, wet fur and all, to his nose.

"This water has that which will feed a plant floating in it."

Jim was quick to describe how, when they had placed the square in the controls above, the plants had answered and then the water had turned brown.

Ana sat down and curled her tail tip over her paws. "This growing thing gives the metal in exchange for special food. It has been taught to do this, I think."

Micha nodded. "And the metal—maybe that comes from the water itself—the People did many strange things—perhaps even with plants."

"What!" Jim exploded. "How does it get metal out of the water?"

"By some process in its own body. We know that plants in the ground take food that they need out of the earth. Long have our own people planted certain things which we need for food. The plants are so many and of such different kinds that, once their products are put in our food machines, they can satisfy us and keep us well without the need for killing. . . . Your people killed to eat." Micha made a sound as if that idea was very bad indeed.

118

"Now here is a plant," he continued, "that is more than a plant. This plant's kin once worked for the People. Though they have been gone a long time, it seems that the plants of this kind did not die out. Somehow they passed the memory of the summons and the rich food to follow. So they came when you once more called them. And they will come for us. We have much to learn about the People, we know. But this is a great discovery, a very great discovery."

"What about those nasty crabs?" Elly Mae asked.

"We routed them with the sound we made. Perhaps there is a way of making a sound continue about this island which will send them off into places where they cannot attack the plants. Until we learn how to do that we shall put a patrol here—a patrol of our loudest voiced Ka'ats. Now, show us this place where you discovered the means of calling the plants."

Elly Mae did not turn at once. Instead she walked over to the plant. She was try-

119

ing very hard to think-talk with it. The plant person stood straight, its leaf eyes turned in her direction. She wanted to let it know they were truly friends. Then. . . .

Just as before she had felt fear and pain—so now—now she felt good inside! Maybe the plant people could not make sounds, nor think-talk—but they could feel and she could *feel* with them!

"Strange," Fledyi mind-said, "the cubling can understand. I get nothing of what she thinks she feels."

"I feel it, too," Jim exclaimed. "It—it feels safe now and it wants us to know that."

"You have been hands for us," Fledyi said, "because you are like the People in your bodies. Now you must be those who talk with the plants for us—for that gift we do not have either."

Elly Mae put out her hand. But she did not quite touch the leaves now standing well up and away from the thick stem body.

"It—I think it likes us—all of us," she

120

said slowly. "It likes us enough to want to be here where we are."

"Good enough," Ana though briskly. "Now let us see just what can be done with this place of the People. It is another one of their secrets which may be worth very much to all of us, Ka'at-kin."

They were going into the tunnel, but Elly Mae still held back, looking at the plant. Now she gave it a wave of her hand.

"Don't you never mind none," she told it.

Maybe it did not understand her words, but she was very sure it understood her feeling. "We're gonna be here to fix things, so you don't never have to be afraid again."

There was a feeling in answer—such a good feeling—and the plant bobbed its two eye leaves in a slow, deep wave as Elly Mae turned to hurry after the others.